I0581215

Bernadette McComish

Florence Nightingale's Lost Log

LILY POETRY REVIEW BOOKS

Published by Lily Poetry Review Books
223 Winter Street
Whitman, MA 02382

https://lilypoetryreview.blog/

ISBN: 978-1-7365990-8-2

Published in the United States by Lily Poetry Review Books.
Library of Congress Control Number: 2021941657

Cover design: Martha McCollough
Cover image: *Florence Nightingale an angel of mercy.* Coloured mezzotint, c. 1855, by Tomkins after Butterworth. Courtesy Wikimedia Commons

The following collection is in the voice of Florence Nightingale during the Crimean War (1854-1856). Throughout her life there is no evidence of a long-term romantic relationship. In these journal entries she encounters a love affair that may have existed but has never been told.

Contents

Before Scutari[1]

4 November 1854

We await our fate
on wind, wood, and wave.

I stagger upon deck.
Through the dense mist I see
the plains of Troy
the tomb of Achilles—

I do not question his weakness
even with his status among the Gods.

The battle, like love
better in our dreams.

A storm prepares us—
400 wounded waiting on shore.

The old Gods peered down,
drowned us in their violent tears.

Trojan ghosts whisper
give up your fever for heroes.

It's true; wars do not stop for stories.

Battle of Inkerman[2]
16 November 1854

They began to flood in from the coast.
Blood, and more gore, every man missing
a leg, an arm or an eye. Not even
bandages made from torn shirts;
no tourniquets.

The only thing
I could see or taste
was mud, and blood—
high on my sleeves.

When they brought him,
his left leg—

He didn't cry out, or flinch—

his name, James—

I didn't have to know,

his needs—

his leg had to be amputated
he would have to lie on that wooden table in the forest.
We would saw it
hack through the crushed bone.

His single sodden boot—

inventoried.

His leg—

piled with others for fire.

Sleepless

22 November 1854

In the Kingdom of Hell[3]—
four miles of beds
eighteen inches apart.

That first night—

one man said,
I was dreaming of my friends at home,
and James said, *and I was thinking.*

I am no spy
but I listen to the men
six limbs between them;

I must rebuild; these soldiers
are dreamers.

Dying Me

23 November 1854

Barrack mistress
attending 3600 wounded
from Balaclava

consequence follows cause
after autumn comes winter

from the Purveyor's store, I take

1 needle
474 Cotton shirts
55 bedpans
200 drinking cups
55 water cans
1 hand broom
5 hair brooms
5 candlesticks
2 table knives
3000 tin plates
6 packages of nails[4]

nothing like figures to be impressive

they anchor, they firm

truth is ruined in the pocket
only the actor succeeds
the originator perishes without credit

Desolation

20 November 1854

I dress what's left of his leg;
the gangrene gone.

It's the first time he's seen
a clean sponge or blanket he tells me.

He says he likes to watch the girls mop,

he's lucky to have a bed
the less sick sleep on beds of earth.

I made him a stump pillow
a small J on the corner—

no other nurse's needlepoint compares.

Used

The meat has been raw
and the water has not been
boiled.[5] I have ordered
the meat to be cooked and boned—

4,000 men were given gristle
or bone, and one night an infected,
cut-up, sheep ended up in James's ward all night.

I toil my way into the confidence
of medical men and soldiers alike,

I'm no surgeon, but his limb looked
as if it might grow back. I pretend
it's possible, I say, if men lived
as long as trees.

Eve

23 December 1854

I watch him toss
as if he had two legs.
He's lucky to have his eyes,
so many men are blind,
I tell him.

He says God would never
have taken his eyes,
not before he had the chance to see
my face at night.

He is the only one
who's ever asked,
what's on my mind.
I never tell,
instead I recite lists,
lists of supplies, lists of new patients,
lists of those who died.

He never frowns, or cries,
only asks me more
about me, my favorite food,
I don't have one,
favorite color, white,
favorite flower,
flowers die too soon,
I say, and he just laughs
and promises to send white roses
when he gets home.

Presents[6]

Xmas Day 1854

Socks 1000 prs.
Flannel 10,000 yrds. (or flannel shirts)
Slippers 2000 prs. (Warm shoes for the troops)
Soap ad libitum (the soap here is not good)
Knives & Forks & Spoons (3000 more)
Cocoa Nut Matting with the long pile such as is used for mats to
clean feet in Workhouses. (By feet of Orderlies, our *Sick* corridors
become like muddy roads.)
Air Cushions 100— fifty round with a hole in the middle— for
bedsores.
(8) Chocolate

Myth

2 January 1855

There is no recovery in today's report,
and the old Gods would laugh if I uttered
regret. My long unwilling silence
is the only evidence I'll have left
when his fever returns.

What strange mercy I sew with dull pins,
how silly these patients would think of my
girlish embroidery.

I'd trade a fortnight of rations for a piece of melon
or a delicate ribbon for my hair.

He's never seen me without boots
caked with Poseidon's grief: salt, water, earth.

Convalescence

3 January 1855

The vermin that come in and out
could carry off the barracks on their backs.

Bandage, wrap, cut, tape, eat,
cook, sew, scrub, count, bandage, cut, blood, then sleep.

I watched James tear his meal
like a dog who hasn't been fed;

no forks, no knives.

Tomorrow I don my lion's skin again.

Scutari[7]

25 January 1855

The crying doesn't keep me awake,
no time for a good novel
no time to let him kiss my shadow—

he will be there in the morning, ready to be fed,
bathed, wounds dressed
he will not shy away,
he will welcome warm water, my hands,
and I must not let him know that although I pretend
to be a nurse all day,
I'm secretly his.

The sponge will not satisfy but the water

and iodine keep us clean.

Winter

5 February 1855

A new batch
of frostbitten stretcher cases arrived
from trench duty today.

We bury every 24 hours.
When we settle
and the air is free from dust,

the mostly murdered can not march in—

exposed bones covered in white frost,
and the blood returns,
this time from Sevastopol.

This winter's work will not have room for dreams,
it will be taking off
ice dead feet, and closing
eyes frozen open.

Night Pieces

15 February 1855

I fold clean
linen in perfect squares;

stack shirts separate
from medical supplies.

I used to dislike
disinfecting saws and syringes.

Today, I soap silver
and smell metal hands

finally free from blood,
calluses pruned to pulp.

I dry my thumbs,
tuck them into my apron,

when day soaks
into night, I know

the Sandman is near
but he will not steal my eyes.

My routine is regular
not mechanical

I am flesh and fluid—
palpable and ready for bed.

Conditions

2 March 1855

Even after the roof came off again and again, my heart
would not break from disappointment

There are not enough pillows,
no linens left. I fear nothing
can be done and everything
done is a failure.

So perish those who pioneer
the way for Mankind.

Give me more myrrh,
and less flesh.

Brutum Fulmen[8]

27 April 1855[9]

My avatar, my owl
Athena[10] came along the cliff
and squawked her song
of more deterioration:

struggle is useless,

then she fled—

the shade of Ajax.

Spring

8 May 1855

Nothing blooms but the sky—
the purest sapphire
one deep, dark blue—

The sea glassy calm—

one star rising above Constantinople.

Confrontation

2 June 1855

Appendages left like chicken parts
taken to the fire. Smoke and prayer
cover corridors like skin clings to sinew.

Men with no arms,
or eyes. Tonight I could end in a sick
bed of my own. I used to dream

of faceless love. Today, rats eat through
gauze while I clean extremities,
saws, and scalpels. No amount of lye
can kill war—

a bacteria I can not combat.

Mortality

12 July 1855

The soldiers are drunk again,
40 women
among 3000 men
complicates recovery.

In Sickness as in Health[11]

18th July 1855

A Serjt. picked me a nosegay
and said,

Had I been with you,
this would not have happened.

I do not believe these men could keep
themselves from fighting. Their bodies
flayed, bullets lodged in fractured skulls
psyche still intact.

When I lie down, which I never do
I dream of James, wish away desire.

Not one flirtation,
I lie in letters.

I Baptize myself in fire,
a would be savior
and he is my disciple
begging me to betray
my assignment.

I suffer from a compound fracture
of my intellect.

Kadikoi[12]

27 August 1855

At 4 am I heard James
call my name, his hand
stretched out, he stood tall,
and called, *Flo, Flo*, but
as I woke, someone screamed, *the hospital is on fire.*

If the wind had been stronger
it might have been true, but it was Kadikoi
across the sea,

with stillness fire spread in one hour,
the town one blazing sheet
of orange smoke. Even now the sky remains
one hue of flame.

the lone sound—
an occasional dog howling
at the cold full moon
reflected in the black Bosphorus.

Almost

4 September 1855

He survived for weeks
on champagne wine alone,
I've never seen
such another case.

He forgot balance
with one leg,
trades his rations
for brandy.

His bedsores worsened
and he said he missed
silk, we had only
linen in hospital life.

I prayed he would
find a road to his maxim—
let *the wind*
blow over him.

No soul could take
charge of my poor corrupted
merchant sailor, soldier,
amputee and watchmaker.

While I was ill
another nurse found his fever
had returned, she asked

Where shall you go to
when you die?
and he replied,
To Miss Nightingale's.

Although now I am
a captive in my own bed
I am thankful the mercy of God has
been shown him.

To Be Penelope

29 October 1855

23

In my fever sleep
I see his unshaven face
an axe in hand
ready to split a trunk

his mouth moves, he tries
to tell me something
his lips shape Olive
and I almost hear the O.

Did he plan to build me
a bed, how fine to see a one legged man
chop down a tree, leave home
a soldier, return
a carpenter, *I live, he says,* and now

he is far away, in some field
unable to move
I think I hear him call
Olive, I live, I love.

Citation

Florence Nightingale: Letters from the Crimea 1854-1856, edited by Sue M. Goldie; pp. 326. Manchester and New York: Mandolin, 1997; distributed by St. Martin's Press.

Notes

1 Inspired by a letter to her family from Constantinople, on board the Vectis.

2 The Battle of Inkerman took place on November 5th 1854, and shortly after almost 3,000 soldiers arrived at Scutari hospital where Florence Nightingale waited with only forty other nurses. In her letter to Dr. William Bowman on November 14th 1854 she writes in detail and states, "we have not an average of three limbs per man." (36-37)

3 Inspired by her letter to Dr. William Bowman on November 14th 1854 where she writes, "…but this is the Kingdom of Hell, no doubt," and that "We now have four miles of beds—and not eighteen inches apart."

4 Inspired by her letter to Sidney Herbert on December 21st 1854." (52)

5 Inspired by her letter to Sidney Herbert on January 8th 1855 she writes, "…the meat is not cooked, the water is not boiled…" (71)

6 Inspired by her letter to Sidney Herbert, Xmas day 1854 where she lists the things they need. (59)

7 The Barrack Hospital at Scutari was Florence Nightingale's base during the Crimean War. It is now called Üsküdar.

8 Latin phrase meaning an insensible thunder bolt; also, a futile threat or display of force.

9 Inspired by a letter to her family, March 5th 1855. (102)

10 Florence Nightingale kept a pet owl named Athena.

11 Inspired by her letter to Parthenope, May 10th, 1855, and her letter to her family June 18th 1855.

12 Kadikoi was a village on the Crimean peninsula in the 19th century. Inspired by her letter to Bracebridges, August 27th 1855. (146)

Acknowledgments

"Almost" was published in *Hospital Drive, The Literature and Humanities Journal of the University of Virginia's School of Medicine.* Issue 8, summer 2012.

"Sleepless," "Eve," "Winter," and "Night Pieces" were published in *The Cortland Review,* Issue 50, February 2011.

ABOUT THE AUTHOR

Born in a blizzard in NY with the gifts of premonition and manifestation, Bernadette McComish is an educator and fortuneteller. She earned an M.F.A. from Sarah Lawrence, and an M.A. in TESOL from Hunter College. Her poems have appeared in The Cortland Review, For Women Who Roar, Slipstream, Flypaper Magazine, Peregrine, and she was a finalist for the New Millennium Writers 41st poetry prize. Her chapbook— *The Book of Johns* was published in 2018 by Dancing Girls Press. She teaches High School in LA, and performs poetry and produces shows with The Poetry Society of New York making poetry accessible to everyone.

Links:

IG: https://www.instagram.com/berndecember/?hl=en
Facebook: https://www.facebook.com/bernadette.mccomish/